The Flying Bed

NANCY WILLARD

paintings by

JOHN THOMPSON

THE BLUE SKY PRESS • AN IMPRINT OF SCHOLASTIC INC. • NEW YORK

For Bonnie, who asked for the story
N. W.

To my wife, Darren, and my daughter, Ryan, for their love and support
throughout the five years it took to create these paintings

To Bonnie for her vision and patience

Special thanks to Syracuse University, Claudia and her family
at Mastro Fornaio di Durrazzi, Stefania Talini,
Meagan Arbital, Craig Roth, and Scott Connor
J. T.

THE BLUE SKY PRESS

Library of Congress catalog card number: 2005000689
ISBN 13: 978-590-25610-0 / ISBN 10: 0-590-25610-6
10 9 8 7 6 5 4 3 2 1   07 08 09 10 11
Printed in Singapore   46
First printing, March 2007
Designed by Kathleen Westray

IN THE CITY OF FLORENCE, ON THE STREET OF ST. AGOSTINO,

lived Guido the baker and his wife, Maria, who, though they worked day and night, earned scarcely enough money to live on. They ate meat only once a week, and the baker owned no winter coat and rarely allowed himself the luxury of a newspaper. They lived in a two-room flat over the shop. Every night after work they climbed fifty-three steps to reach it and told themselves that what they spent in breath they saved in cash, as the top rooms rented for less than rooms more comfortably located.

Maria did, however, drop a handful of change into the alms box of San Spirito at Christmas and Easter, for you can always find people whose need is greater than your own, and her need had taught her to remember theirs.

The shop had belonged to Guido's father, known as Francesco the Joyful because he sang while he worked. Those who remember him claimed that his cheesecakes surpassed anything you and I shall ever see, in this world or the next. *Ting-a-ling!* called the bell over the shop door, all day long. People came from miles away to buy his *Colomba di Probuzione*, the sweet raisin bread sprinkled with almonds and sugar he baked only for Easter. And though he received offers to bake in the big hotels and restaurants for better pay, he always refused, for he wanted to keep his shop in the family.

His son inherited the shop but not, alas, the skill to run it. Guido's icings were lumpy and his fresh bread tasted stale. When he filled the showcases, he mixed the day-old cookies with the fresh ones, instead of cutting the price as his father had done. He skimped on the raisins and left out the almonds and sugar, and the dough he made was heavy and without flavor.

Soon, even the most loyal customers took their business elsewhere. Money grew scarce, and, piece by piece, Guido sold the furniture.

One night, Maria trudged upstairs after a day of sweeping and scrubbing the floors, scouring the oven and the cupboards, and mending the torn pockets in Guido's trousers and the holes in her best sweater. She opened the door and saw no bed.

"Enough is enough!" she shouted. "I can't sleep without a bed. A bed I want and a bed I'll have!"

Guido shook his head.

"I can't even buy a winter coat and you want a bed?"

But she pestered and pleaded and at last she announced she would move back to her father's house until Guido agreed to buy a bed.

"And don't scrimp," she warned him. "It's got to be big enough for both of us."

Very well, a double bed it would be, but not a new one. The week before Maria's birthday, which fell in March, Guido set out in search of a bed small in price but big enough for two. He walked streets he knew and streets he didn't know till the shops closed for the afternoon. To half a dozen shuttered windows he said, "Where, oh where can I find a bed?" The words had scarcely left his mouth when he glanced down a small street that ended at the entrance to a shop unlike any he had ever seen.

The door stood ajar.

Above the door hung a sign.

Painted on the sign was a bed.

For a moment, Guido could scarcely believe his luck. He ran down the street and rushed into the shop, and just in time, too, for no sooner had he set foot inside than the door clicked behind him, and he found himself in a room crammed from tip to top with beds.

Big beds, little beds, bunk beds, junk beds, trundle beds, canopied beds, beds with four posts, beds with no posts. In the middle of the shop, a large woman slouched over a card table on which was spread a game of solitaire. Her feet rested on an electric heater that glowed and hummed. There was no other sound in the room.

Guido walked among high beds and low beds, new beds and broken beds, but even the broken beds cost more money than he kept in his pocket. He did not tell this to the woman, however, who laid down her cards and stared at him.

"Have I seen all your beds?" he asked.

"I've only one other. It's out in back. Believe me, you're better off without it."

"Expensive, eh?" said Guido.

"You can have it for nothing," said the woman. "I won't sell it and I can't keep it. I've sold it twice already, and it always comes back."

"What's wrong with it?"

"How should I know? The last two people who slept there died of fright. And it's a beautiful bed, too. Made by an artist. Do you want to see it?"

Guido nodded and followed her to a second room, which was nearly empty. In the middle of the room stood a bed.

Ah, what a bed! The four posts were carved to match the crisscross texture of palm bark, and a wreath of carved lilies joined the tops of the posts.

"Notice the gold rings on the wreath for hanging the curtains," said the woman.

No curtains hung there now. On the carved headboard gleamed apples so real that what your eye saw, your hand reached for. When Guido touched one, he saw a lantern and a goblet and the faces of three little girls carved into the deep space between the leaves. The woman was watching him.

"Every chair, every spoon, every carpet wants to be admired, but only a few manage it," said the woman. "This bed chooses its owners, and it has chosen you."

The baker felt weak with longing. He rapped the headboard and the footboard, and the woman watched him and shook her head. No, no, she wouldn't part with it. But would he sign a paper absolving her of all guilt if he met with the same fate as the previous owners? Then she would agree to let him take it.

So they sealed the bargain. She would have the bed delivered that very day. Guido hurried home and told Maria about the beautiful carving on the bed and how the bed had chosen him.

"I never heard of a bed choosing the buyer," exclaimed Maria.

"Every chair, every bed, every carpet wants"—Guido tried to remember what the woman had said—"to be set free, but only a few manage it."

He did not mention the fate of the two previous owners.

At twilight, a truck stopped in front of the shop. Five strong women hauled the bed and a mattress up the fifty-three steps to the bedroom of Guido and Maria. Though the bed was large and the room small, it looked as if it had been waiting all its life to be placed in this very spot.

"What did you pay for it?" Maria whispered.

"Nothing," said Guido. "The woman in the shop said, 'This bed chooses its owners, and it has chosen you.' She saw my need and she gave me the bed."

Right away Maria began to polish the bed. And now listen to what a wonderful bed it was: The more she polished the carving the more she saw: a goblet here, a lantern there, the laughing faces of three little girls. She couldn't stop praising her husband's good luck, and as she chattered, her eyes shone, and Guido watched and felt something like pride.

But presently, he felt sleepy.

"Maria, I can't sleep if you stay up all night polishing."

So Maria fetched her best sheets and made up the bed, and the two climbed into it.

Outside the window, the voices of passersby stopped as abruptly as if someone had switched them off. All at once Guido felt such a jiggling and a piggling under him that he nearly tumbled to the floor. But he managed to grab the sheet and pull himself back as he shouted, "Wife! Wife! The bed is waking up!"

Maria sat up, terrified, and pulled the blankets to her chin. The bed was running around and around the room like a pony in a ring. When it caught sight of the open window, it reared up and rushed toward it. The baker might have jumped to safety if his wife hadn't grabbed his arm and held him back.

"Hang on!" she shouted. "A bed I want and a bed I'll have, even if it carries me to the ends of the earth."

Has a bed ears? It bucked once, twice, and sprang out the window, straight into the sky.

When Guido peered down through the darkness, he saw the tiled rooftops of Florence and the great dome of the cathedral growing smaller and smaller. The lights of the city shrank to tiny points and winked out, and the wind teased him and tossed him and froze him, for Maria had rolled herself up in the bedclothes and left him nothing but his pillow. He shouted at her, and she shouted back at him, but neither heard the other over the roar of the wind.

Suddenly the wind dropped, and the bed floated as softly as a petal
on a pond. Guido lifted his head. He heard a strumming here and a
thrumming there, and all round them in the deep blue fields of the sky
blew the bright, blossoming stars.

Ahead of them shone the lights of a town. But what town could it be?
And who were these barefoot men and women in white aprons, who

caught the bed and stroked it and said, "What a good bed you are! What a good bed you are!"

The bed stood still, but it did not turn into one of those quiet beds you and I sleep in. No, it kept shifting its legs, as if it were treading water.

Behind the bed shone a crystal oven, and the baker saw tray upon tray of golden loaves on the racks. The fragrance of freshly baked bread hung in the air.

"Are there kitchens in the sky?" Guido exclaimed.

The master baker, a huge man with flour on his bare feet and butter on his beard, stepped forward.

"Many look for me, but few find me. Who are you?"

Guido and Maria climbed out of bed and bowed, for his great size seemed to demand it.

"I am a poor baker," said Guido. "The poorest baker on earth."

And hearing himself say this, he could hardly hold back his tears. The master baker's face showed neither surprise nor pity.

"I knew your father, Francesco the Joyful," he mused. "When he baked the Easter bread, he was generous with the raisins and the almonds and the sugar."

Guido shrugged. "He was lucky and I'm not. Whatever I touch turns against me."

"Ah," said the master baker. He was silent for a long time. His assistants moved to and fro, as if on feathered feet, opening and closing the oven door as silently as snow.

Then the master baker drew from his apron a little cheesecloth bag.

"Some call me luck, some call me fate. Take this yeast. Use it when you bake your bread. Never again will you and your wife go hungry."

And he pressed it into Guido's palm.

"Thank you," said Maria and Guido with one voice.

"My gifts come only once in a lifetime, and they do not come to everyone. Now, listen carefully."

The bread listened, the assistants listened, even the stars brightened with attention.

"Tell nobody about this gift, or it will be as worthless as a cracked cup," said the master baker. "Go home now, and don't forget what I've told you."

Has a bed eyes? It fled across the sky as if it had a map and set the baker and his wife down in their own room. They lay there, clutching each other's hands, and both felt the weight of the cold bag of yeast between them. Maria rubbed her eyes.

"So it wasn't a dream. Let's get up at once and bake the bread."

They dressed quickly and hurried downstairs to the kitchen. Together they hauled out the last sack of flour and mixed the dough, and the baker opened the bag of yeast and poured out a fine, silvery powder that dusted the dough, sank into it, and disappeared, like snow on a spring day.

Guido shut the bag of yeast, tied it at the neck, and tucked it into a small crock, which he hid on a shelf in the pantry. Then he sat down opposite his wife to a breakfast of coffee and stale bread and waited for the dough to rise.

Whee! It rose so fast that you and I would have thought the master baker was inside, blowing it out like a balloon. Guido and Maria watched in amazement. When it stopped growing, Guido jumped up and clapped his hands.

"Come, let's shape the loaves," he exclaimed. "This is truly marvelous bread."

They cut the dough and patted it, and it seemed to them that they had seven times as much as they'd had before.

Now, the fragrance of bread baking is wonderful, but the fragrance of this bread was divine. It rolled into the street and into the houses; no door could keep it out. Like the national anthem, it brought people to their feet. Like a parade, it hustled them out of their homes. At the end of the day, Guido counted more coins in his till than he usually earned in a week.

After supper he was so tired that he went straight to bed, and Maria climbed in beside him. The bed gave a little hop of joy, waltzed twice around the room, nuzzled up to the window, pushed open the shutters, and sprang into the night sky. This time, it circled the city of Florence, flying so low they could see their reflections in the Arno, the river that runs through the city. Over the bridges they flew, pausing over the shuttered stalls of the goldsmiths on the Old Bridge, then darting like a dragonfly toward the city gates and the villas beyond, with their terraced gardens and grottoes and fountains. Around and around it flew, in wider and wider circles, till the baker and his wife fell asleep from exhaustion.

The next morning they found themselves in their own room with the sun pouring through the open shutters.

Guido jumped up and shouted, "It's nearly noon, and the bread's not even started! No more gallivanting around at night in this bed."

"But where will we sleep?" asked Maria.

"Tonight we sleep on the floor. Tomorrow, I'll look for another bed."

"I want this one," said Maria.

"What for? We can't get a wink of sleep."

Squeak! Squeak! The bed was tiptoeing toward the open window.

"Lock the shutters," said Guido. "I'm going back to the store and ask the woman to take the bed back."

He walked streets he knew and streets he didn't know, but he could not find the small street that ended at the entrance to the shop that sold beds.

In the afternoon, when the shops closed, he returned to the kitchen and baked the Easter bread, and he remembered to be generous with the raisins and the almonds and the sugar. He did not forget to add a pinch of yeast from the bag hidden in a crock on a shelf in the pantry.

That night, Guido stood at one end of the bed and Maria stood at the other, and they pulled off the mattress, yanked off sheets and pillows and blankets, and spread them on the floor. The baker fell asleep right away and dreamed he was a child in the kitchen many years ago, dozing on the little nap-bed his mother made for him out of two chairs so that she could watch him as she rolled frosting into roses for the wedding cakes. But Maria couldn't sleep. She could hear the bed pacing up and down in front of the locked window.

Day after day, week after week, the baker worked late and rose early, and the money rolled in. He bought a freezer for keeping the ice cream cold and ordered *gelato* in ten different flavors to fill it, and the customers lined up for it. There was pistachio and hazelnut and tangerine and passion fruit and flavors so new no one had invented a name for them yet.

"A new bed we need and a new bed we'll have," he said to Maria. "Why should people with money sleep on the floor?"

"Where will we find a new bed as beautiful as this carved one?" exclaimed Maria.

But that evening, after a long day's work, they saw a brand-new bed: plain, unadventurous, and comfortable.

The carved one stood in the room with nothing to wear but empty golden rings. When Maria felt weary at the end of the day, she would polish it and polish it till she saw the carved apples and the lantern and the goblet and the laughing faces of the three little girls. And when the bed glowed with its old splendor, she felt rested and happy and went to sleep singing to herself while Guido tossed and turned and muttered in his sleep: "More money, more money!"

Oh, the smell of money was in the air! Orders for wedding cakes arrived daily. The whole town seemed bent on marriage. The baker and his wife rose at three each morning and stirred, pounded, baked, and sweated in the kitchen till seven, when the customers began to arrive. The shop bell rang all day long, *ting-a-ling, ting-a-ling!* until Guido tied a rag around the clapper to silence it. Maria filled the orders, wrapped them, rang up the change, and ran to and fro, toting trays of rolls and cookies and bread from the kitchen to the showcases, and the faster she ran the louder she hissed between her teeth at Guido, "Are we machines? Are we slaves? Let's hire someone to help us."

And Guido said, "Why should we give our money to strangers?"

The next morning, Maria was too tired to get up. She lay shivering under the quilt and refused to dress.

"What can I bring you to make you feel better?" Guido asked.

"Apples," she whispered. "I would like apples as beautiful as the ones on our bed."

Guido's heart sank. He could not run the shop without her, and yet he could not close it. He crept downstairs in the darkness, lit the ovens, and rolled out the dough for *pignoli* cookies. He did not have time to go shopping for apples.

Ting-a-ling! The shop bell startled him. Guido wiped his hands on his apron and hurried into the shop and snapped on the overhead light. On the other side of the counter stood an elegant stranger in a black coat and a black fur hat that made him look taller than he really was. Guido was about to say, "The shop doesn't open till seven," until he saw the diamond rings that the stranger wore on each finger. The jewels winked at Guido as if they were letting him in on a joke, and he heard himself say, "May I help you?"

The stranger smiled and began to speak, slowly and patiently, as if he were teaching a parrot to talk.

"I own a large restaurant, and I need a master baker."

Guido scratched his head.

"I can't leave my shop. It's a family business. It must stay in the family."

"You have children?"

"No, not yet."

The stranger twirled first one ring, then another ring, then another ring, until the whole shop glittered with a hard, bright light.

"I do not know the secret of your excellent baking, but I know you have one, for three months ago you were a failure, and now you have no equal among all the bakers in Florence. If I can't buy your services, will you sell me your secret? You can name your own price."

Silence.

"Two million lire? Paid in cash, of course."

Two million lire! The baker hesitated, but only for a moment.

"The secret is in the yeast," he said.

"Ah," said the stranger. "Will you sell me your yeast?"

"I can't sell all of it," said the baker.

"I don't need all of it," said the stranger.

On hearing this, the baker fetched his bag of yeast from the crock in the pantry, measured a tablespoonful into an envelope, and put the envelope into the stranger's hands.

"Now give me my money."

"Of course," said the stranger.

He drew from his coat pocket a wad of bills and counted them into

the baker's hand.

Two million lire.

From that hour forward, everything turned out badly. Guido paid for five sacks of flour with one of the stranger's bills, and the next day the police arrested him for paying with counterfeit money. A careful inspection of his good fortune revealed it to be worthless.

After he'd paid the fine, there was scarcely enough left for the baker and his wife to live on. They ate meat only once a week, and Guido sold his *gelato* freezer and rarely allowed himself the luxury of a newspaper. The freshly baked bread turned stale on the rack, and soon even the most loyal customers took their business elsewhere. Maria no longer dropped a handful of change into the alms box of San Spirito, for she could not imagine anyone whose need was greater than theirs.

Winter came early, and Guido could not afford a winter coat.

"Tomorrow I'm going to chop up the old bed for firewood," he announced. "Fate is against us."

That night after Guido was fast asleep, Maria crept out of the new bed, climbed into the old one, and pulled the mattress onto the broken springs. The bed stretched its legs, shook itself, and trotted up to the window. Maria unlocked the shutters, which closed behind her, and the icy wind rushed in and sank its teeth into her.

"Take me to the master baker," whispered Maria.

Out of the window sprang the bed, over the city of Florence into the dark sky. Maria hung on, past five planets and the Northern Lights, and just when she thought she would die of cold, she spied the lights and towers of the master baker's town, and her spirits soared.

"Soon I'll be warm again," she told herself.

But alas! The faster the bed flew toward it, the faster the town flew away. The poor bed creaked and cracked till Maria feared it was falling to pieces, and all this while the lights shrank to a hazy band, and the master baker's town glided farther and farther away.

"Oh, bed, bed, take me home," whispered Maria, leaning her cheek against the carved apples. "Take me home, and I promise you that I will not lock the window tonight. Take me home, and I will not let Guido burn you."

The bed spun around and sank slowly, slowly, toward the earth, and Maria caught the smell of apples.

The goblet was full of cider and nestled itself in her hand.

The lantern lit its candle and warmed her cheek.

She woke up in her own room with Guido snoring by her side. In her right hand she held the lantern, which had not gone out. In her left hand she held the goblet, which was empty but still fragrant. The light of the full moon showed her, piled on the floor all around the bed, the most beautiful apples she had ever seen.

Maria jumped out of bed and gathered them into a bowl. People who tell their children the story say there were enough apples to share with all the customers who came into the shop that day, and those apples tasted of almonds and sugar and raisins and honey.

WHAT I AM TELLING YOU HAPPENED A LONG TIME AGO,

and I am sorry to say that if you go to the street of St. Agostino, you will not find the bed. No, you must look for it in the sky, where it lives and travels until it is called for. Look for it just beyond the Big Dipper, when the meteor showers fall in August.

And don't expect to find Guido and Maria running the shop, for they are no longer young, and they've passed it on to their three daughters, who sing while they work and whose cheesecake surpasses anything you and I shall ever see, in this world or the next. They will smile at you and tell you that their good fortune comes from their hands and not from magic.

But if you go there, look for a little cupboard with glass doors to the right of the cash register. If it holds a goblet and a lantern, you will know you are in the right place.

Ask the oldest daughter to unlock it for you.

Ask the middle daughter for a drink of cider from the goblet.

And when you buy a candle from the youngest daughter, ask her to light it from the flame in the lantern. It was from her that I bought mine, and it is by starlight that I write this story.